ZONE 13

The Shape Shifter

DAVID ORME

Ransom

The Shape Shifter
by David Orme
Illustrated by Jorge Mongiovi and Ulises Carpintero
Cover photographs: © Алексей Егоров, Guylaine Brunet

Published by Ransom Publishing Ltd.
Radley House, 8 St. Cross Road, Winchester, Hampshire, SO23 9HX, UK
www.ransom.co.uk

ISBN   978 184167 459 9

First published in 2011

Originally published in 1998 by Stanley Thornes Publishers Ltd.

A CIP catalogue record of this book is available from the British Library.

CONTENTS

1

THE CREATURE ON THE MOOR

It was a cold night on the moor. A few sheep were sheltering behind a pile of rocks. They could feel the cold wind, even through their thick coats.

There was no sound except the wind, but the sheep could sense danger. The moon was nearly full, but they couldn't see anything. Even so, they knew something was out there.

Was it a fox? A fox was no danger to them. The lambs had grown up by now.

A dark creature was padding silently
through the bracken. It could smell the sheep.
In its shining yellow eyes, there was a lust for
blood.

The creature jumped on top of the rocks.
The sheep saw the danger. Too late!

With a snarl, the creature leapt on to the
back of one of the sheep. The rest of the flock
ran down the hillside in terror. The sheep tried

to fight free, but the creature was at its throat.
Soon, the sheep lay still.

The creature ripped open the belly of the
sheep. It pushed its jaws into the hot blood. It
pulled out the liver and intestines with sharp
tugs.

The creature enjoyed its meal, growling
now and then in case any other animal came
near.

Minutes later, the black beast bounded away across the lonely moor.

There was no sound but the wind, and the bleating of the terrified sheep from the bottom of the hill.

THE MEETING

John Pendarren had nearly a thousand acres of land. Most of it was wild moor. This was useless for anything except sheep. When sheep were killed, it was a big blow to John.

Ted Barnes, the local vet, was looking at the body of the sheep. It was in the back of John's 4x4.

'What do you think then, Ted?' asked John. 'I reckon a dangerous dog has got loose. Maybe it was a Pit Bull.'

Ted shook his head.

'I've seen a lot of dog attacks in my time, but this doesn't look like one. Look at these teeth marks on the ribs! They're like the marks made by a big cat.'

John scratched his head.

'I don't believe those stories about a big cat on the moor! What do you think?'

'I'm not sure,' said Ted. 'There are reports of these big cats from all over the place, but

there is no real evidence, or any reports about one escaping from a zoo. No one has managed to take a photo of one, and no dead ones have been found. But this isn't the first sheep I've seen killed like this. It just doesn't make sense.'

Sammy, the farm cat, appeared. He rubbed his back on Ted's boot. Ted bent down and picked him up. He scratched the cat's ears. Sammy loved that.

'Maybe one of your big cousins is out there!' said Ted. 'You'd better watch out. It would have you for breakfast!'

Ted put Sammy down. The cat headed for the barn. There was a family of rats there that needed dealing with.

ANOTHER DEATH

Next day, there was another dead sheep for
John to deal with. It hadn't been killed out on
the moor. It had been attacked in the field
next to the farm. That was really worrying.
John kept sheep that needed extra care in this
field. The dead animal was special – John had
hoped to win a prize with it at the County
Show in Bodmin. The death of the sheep was
a bad blow.

He talked it over with Terry. Terry was
John's shepherd. It was his job to look after
the sheep. He had spent a cold night in a little
hut out on the moor.

'The trouble is, boss, you can't be in two
places at once,' Terry said. 'I really don't know
what the answer is.'

John made a decision.

'I think we'll bring the whole flock down to the home field for a few nights. We'll both sit up and see if we can find out what's going on.'

Terry agreed. That was the best plan.

'What do you reckon it is, boss?'

'I still think it's a dog. We don't believe all this talk about big cats, do we Sammy?'

Sammy had been lying asleep on a wall nearby. He woke up, stretched his legs. He followed John into the farmhouse, hoping for a saucer of milk.

THAT NIGHT

John and Terry decided to take turns. They would watch the sheep for two hours each. When they were off duty, they could doze in the farm kitchen.

They did this for four nights. Nothing happened. The sheep stayed safely in the fields by the farmhouse. On the fifth day, John decided to put the sheep back on the moor.

'If we keep them here, we will have to start feeding them,' he said to Terry.

Terry and his sheep dogs herded the sheep up to the moor.

The next morning, there was bad news. Another sheep was dead.

'It seems to know exactly what we are doing,' said Terry.

That night, John found it difficult to sleep. He was worried about his sheep. He got up late in the night and went for a look around.

He heard a sound from the sheep field. Just a few sheep were left there now. He went across to check on them.

There was just enough moonlight to see a long black shape in the dark. It was creeping across the field towards the sheep! The sheep could sense the animal. They were bleating in panic.

John wished he had brought his shotgun. He jumped over the fence and ran towards the animal. He yelled at it. Its great head turned, and John could see its shining yellow eyes, and heard its snarl.

Suddenly, John felt very afraid. But the animal seemed more frightened of him. It cut back across the field towards the farm. John chased after it.

The barn door was open. John saw the huge black shape slip inside. He rushed over and slammed the door shut. He put a big bar across. The creature was trapped.

TRAPPED!

The next morning, a group of people stood outside the barn.

Terry and John were there, and Ted Barnes, the vet, and the local policeman. John carried a shotgun.

John told everyone the story of the night before.

'It was definitely a big cat,' he said. 'It was too dark to see exactly what sort it was, but it looked really dangerous!'

'When it looked at me with its wicked-looking yellow eyes, I thought it was going to turn on me. I didn't have my shotgun with me. If I had, I would have killed it there and then.

'I thought it would head off to the hills, but it ran into the barn. And it's trapped in there now. There's no other way out.'

Carefully, Terry pulled back the bar and opened the door.

'Careful now, everyone,' John said. 'This creature is a killer. It could be at your throat in seconds.'

Everyone stood ready. John aimed his gun ...

And out of the barn strolled Sammy the cat!

Everyone started laughing. John felt very embarrassed.

'But I know it was there last night,' he said feebly.

ooo//ooo

Late that night, Sammy left the warm kitchen and set off towards the moor. He stopped in the tall bracken. His yellow eyes looked like two full moons.

Slowly, Sammy's body grew longer, his great legs stretched, and his savage teeth glinted in the pale moonlight.

NOT FOR THE PUBLIC TO KNOW
TOP SECRET
ZONE 13 FILES ONLY

ABOUT THE AUTHOR

David Orme is an expert on strange, unexplained events. For his protection (and yours) we cannot show a photograph of him.

David created the Zone 13 files to record the cases he studied. Some of these files really do involve aliens, but many do not. Aliens are not everywhere. Just in most places.

These stories are all taken from the Zone 13 files. They will not be here for long. Read them while you can.

But don't close your eyes when you go to sleep at night. **They** will be watching you.